TWO FACES OF JANUS

A Short Story of Ancient Rome

LINNEA TANNER

Contents

Chapter 1 New Beginnings 1

Chapter 2 Two Faces of Augustus 13

Chapter 3 Room of the Masks...................29

Chapter 4 Forced Suicide...........................37

Chapter 5 Aftermath..................................49

Chapter 6 Sunrise 61

New Beginnings

ON THIS BRIGHT AND SUNNY afternoon, I, Lucius, had the hubris of youth, giving no regard to the memory of my grandfather, Marcus Antonius. Emperor Augustus Caesar had erased his name from all of the public records and had all his statues destroyed by an act of *damnatio memoriae*. Except for the bust that my father, Iullus Antonius, had hidden in our storage cellar.

For me, though, today marked a new beginning—my ascension in the Imperial Court. In his epic poem, I recalled the poet, Ovid, asking the two-faced god Janus about his origin and purpose. Janus, the god of beginnings, replied, "Whatever you see—sky, sea, clouds, earth— all things are closed and opened by my hand. The guardianship of this vast universe is in my hands alone."

Ovid then asked, "Why, Janus, when I placate other gods, do I bring incense and wine to you first?"

"So that you may gain entry to whatsoever gods you wish," Janus replied, "through me because I guard the threshold."

That is how I felt on this cloudless, carefree day. I, like Janus, could open the gateway to my destiny.

The air was redolent with the scent of sweet-smelling roses as I strolled alongside my friend, Gaius Caesar, through the gardens on Aventine Hill. I flipped a gold coin that I had won at the chariot races that morning, but it slipped through my fingertips. Picking it up, I cast a glance at Gaius.

"You should have bet on the green chariot race team," I jested.

Gaius chuckled. "Certainly, Fortuna smiles on you today. Perhaps next time, Lucius, I'll bet on a gladiatorial game instead."

I put the gold coin in my drawstring purse and hid it underneath my belt. "Have you heard more about your military assignment in Armenia?" I asked.

"Not yet," Gaius said, his hand caressing the hilt of his belted gladius. "Some imperial advisors think I'm too young. I train with a freed gladiator, though. What about you? Have you heard about your assignment as a praetor in the courts?"

"I've petitioned Augustus for his patronage," I proudly proclaimed. I was anticipating that the princeps would announce his sponsorship any day. "My mother has spoken to him about supporting my appointment. Perhaps today, he'll summon me to discuss my position. As you say, Fortuna smiles on me today."

"Will you be going to the public baths today?" Gaius asked, unsheathing his gladius. He brashly swung it to and fro, almost nicking me with its tip.

I jumped back to avoid the blade. "Careful with that!" I snapped angrily.

Inexplicably, Gaius steadied the sword's tip near my throat. "Scared?"

Unsettled by the seriousness in my friend's voice, I gently pushed the blunt end of the blade away with my hand. "Should I be?"

Gaius smirked and sheathed his weapon. "Just playing with you. You didn't answer me. Will you be going to the public baths near the Circus Maximus?"

I fisted my hand to keep it still, unsure if it was shaking from fear or from anger that my friend had drawn a sword on me. "My mother asked me to return home today."

Gaius looked up at the sky. A shadow from a storm cloud drifted over us. "Perhaps your mother already knows what my grandfather has in mind for you. Is there still trouble brewing between your parents?"

The change in the direction of Gaius's conversation at first took me aback. Then I remembered that I had spoken to him the previous week about my concerns with my parents. "I've not seen my father in a week. I can't quite put my finger on it, but I fear my parents might divorce."

Gaius raised an eyebrow. "Have they told you so?"

"Neither one has said a word to me. Yet still, I felt the tension in the air when Father was home last week."

My companion's gaze suddenly shifted beyond me to the hilltop steps. "Isn't that your slave, Brigata, approaching us?"

I looked to the stairs where my fair-haired slave, originally from Germania, descended a hilltop abloom with crimson roses. She made my heart race whenever we explored new sexual exploits. She had the most alluring sea-blue eyes—I could drown in them.

"Do you still have sex with her?" Gaius asked.

"We meet in secret places for that," I said, regretting that I had previously disclosed my fondness for a slave on the cusp of womanhood.

"It upsets my mother whenever she finds us together in my bedchamber."

My gaze drifted down to the rolled parchment in Brigata's hand. *Perhaps it's good tidings,* I told myself, shaking off an ominous sense of doom.

Finally reaching us, Brigata humbly bowed her head and handed me the scroll. "Urgent message from your mother. Augustus summons you."

My heart was pounding, and I could barely contain my exhilaration at the thought of finally meeting the powerful imperial ruler to discuss my assignment. Yet, when I regarded Brigata's somber grimace, I couldn't understand why she didn't share in my delight.

"What does the message say? I thought you would at least deliver the news with a smile," my voice cracked.

Brigata obliged me with a smile, but it appeared forced. "I am not privileged to know such things."

"Of course not, you are but a slave," I said with a sour bite in my voice, knowing that she often revealed details of family discord when we were alone, our legs entwined. So that I could speak with her privately, I ended the conversation with Gaius.

"If you would excuse me, I need to meet with your grandfather."

"Of course," Gaius replied, with a friendly slap on the back. "Perhaps it's the good tidings you're expecting."

I burst into a grin, speculating that Augustus might have already revealed to Gaius the exciting news about my assignment. "Perhaps, as you said, Fortuna is smiling on me today."

"Why not share your good fortune with me and read the message aloud?" Gaius urged.

I hesitated, studying his subdued expression. "It is meant for my eyes only. Let us talk tomorrow after I've had a chance to talk with Augustus."

Gaius quirked a thin smile. "Tomorrow, then."

I nodded. "*Valle.*"

Gaius bid me farewell and strode off in the direction of the forum.

With my companion gone, I excitedly slipped my forefinger under the wax seal to open the scroll. It read: *Princeps Augustus Caesar immediately summons you to his villa. Hurry. I am with him now. Your beloved mother.*

It seemed odd that my mother had summoned me to Augustus's villa instead of his office in the forum. But then, I broke out into a grin as a possibility occurred to me.

A banquet to honor me!

My mother, Claudia Marcella Major, was the favorite niece of Augustus, the eldest daughter of his sister, Octavia, and her first husband, Gaius Claudius Marcellus. The prospect of a celebratory dinner at the villa made me wild with excitement. I swooped Brigata into my arms jubilantly. "Augustus wants to see me at his estate! Usually, he announces such positions as mine at his headquarters."

Brigata's expression appeared muted. "I am pleased for you, dominus," she replied flatly.

"Pleased? Is that all you can say? You should rejoice with me," I encouraged as I lifted her hand and twirled her around. "Let us celebrate tonight. Come to my bed and show me what you can do with your tongue as you stroke me."

"What about your mother?" Brigata blurted out, dropping her eyes when I glared. Her throat clutched. "Forgive me, Lucius. I only want our moment together to be special," she said, tears welling in her eyes.

Brigata had a way of softening me with her glistening blue eyes, from which shone her adoration for me—a weakness no Roman noble made of iron would ever admit. As I led her by the hand, I caught a glimpse of a black-spotted yellow butterfly flitting past my head. We ascended the stairs amid the fragrant rose garden. There, I spotted the butterfly again, alighting on a crimson rose in full bloom. The sight of its long tongue searching for nectar between the petals aroused me with erotic images of what I could do to Brigata. Hoping my gesture would sweeten her mood for rougher foreplay that night, I quickly grasped for the butterfly's fluttering wings.

"Let me catch it for you," I said, with all of the enthusiasm I could muster. But then, some nasty bug hiding beneath a rose thorn stung me.

Shocked, I yanked my hand away and cursed the gods.

"Let me see," Brigata cooed, gently opening the palm of my hand to pull out the bee's stinger. She lightly kissed my hand and washed away the burning sting with her tears.

Brigata's gesture moved me, an emotion I seldom felt for someone beneath my status. "What could I give you to make you as happy as me?" I asked impetuously.

"My freedom," she said boldly, forthright with no hesitation.

Lost for words, I could not accept that Brigata would want something more than to be my slave mistress. Slightly irritated by her response, I replied with a smug smile, "But then, I couldn't hold you in my arms. Don't you want to stay with me?"

Voice quivering, she meekly lowered her eyes. "Forgive me, dominus. You often talk about how you will embrace your destiny to rise in Rome…how you will choose your pathway. But what would you do if someone else made that choice for you?"

Unnerved by Brigata's bluntness, I gripped her shoulders. "Is there something you're not telling me?"

"I saw fear in your mother's eyes as she handed me the message," Brigata confessed. "But I sense no more than that."

I looked away, perplexed by the mixed signs of the two faces that Janus had shown me that day and the direction of Fortuna's steering oar.

2

Two Faces of Augustus

I DECIDED TO HURRY HOME ON my way to Augustus's residence to change into formal attire. To my surprise, the praetorian prefect, Quintus Scapula, greeted Brigata and me at the door instead of the porter.

"Come inside," he said, with a sweeping gesture of his arm.

When I entered the atrium, six other men attired in white togas were there, one of which I recognized as Augustus's bodyguard. Looking around, I only observed a few male slaves in front of the tablinum, but there was no sign of the porter, who usually answered the door. Uneasy, I turned to Quintus.

"Why is the imperial guard here?" I asked.

"Augustus Caesar asked me to escort you to your meeting with him, in case your mother's message did not reach you," Quintus answered.

"I assume my mother is already with the princeps," I said, aware of the stern frown on the praetorian prefect's face.

"Yes. She is there now."

"Is it usual protocol for you to escort supplicants to meet with Augustus?" I inquired, still uneasy with the praetorian prefect's presence.

"There has been unrest in the city. It is for your safety," Quintus assured me.

"Can I at least change into something more befitting of the meeting?" I requested.

Quintus exchanged a glance with one of the guards. "Be quick. You don't want to keep Caesar waiting."

With Brigata, I strode to my bedchamber toward the back corner of the atrium; a guard followed behind me and waited at the doorway as I dressed.

"Were the guards here before?" I whispered.

"Yes, but I thought they were nobles," Brigata answered as she draped the white toga off my shoulder and wrapped it around my body.

Keeping my voice low, I divulged my trepidation to Brigata. "I don't understand why Augustus sent his praetorian guards to escort me. Did my mother say anything out of the ordinary?"

Brigata shook her head as she smoothed out the wrinkles in the toga.

"It's probably nothing but..." I bit off the words, "it feels as if I'm going to my execution." Then, thinking aloud, I continued, "On further thought, if it were something more, the guards wouldn't allow me to change."

Brigata gave me a perplexed look.

"Never mind." I waved her away. "I must be more anxious about meeting Augustus than I realized," I muttered to myself.

"I'll be here for you tonight," Brigata said, placing her hand on mine—a look of concern on her face.

The gesture relaxed me. Ignoring the guard watching us, I kissed her on the cheek. "How do I look?"

"You look splendid, dominus," she said, stealing a glance at the guard at the door. It irritated me that Brigata could not be more exuberant about her compliment, but then I recognized that as a slave, she was constantly on guard not to show her true feelings. So I told her to wait in the bedchamber until after everyone left.

Striding back to the atrium, I noticed that my father's statue was no longer with the other prestigious family statues—those of my mother, my grandmother Octavia, and her daughters sired by Marcus Antonius—that lined the wall near the doorway to the outside street. A guard diverted my attention when he cleared his throat. "We'd best be going."

"Yes. Of course." I nodded.

Four guards, one on each side of me and one each in front and back, escorted me up the Palatine Hill to Augustus's residence located above the legendary sacred cave, the Lupercal, where the she-wolf suckled the twin founders of Rome. Though many Romans considered the two-level home modest for a politician of Augustus's status, the frescoes and architectural design were considered some of the best in the Roman world.

As I approached the royal residence, I noted pink tinges of the sunset reflecting off the colonnaded Temple of Apollo. Two other armed guards, waiting at the large entrance doors of Augustus's villa, escorted me into the atrium. Several slaves were on their knees scrubbing mosaic tile around the pool set under the compluvium, the aperture in the roof. One, a short-statured slave with a shiny bald spot in his thinning gray hair, directed us to a staircase leading to the second floor.

With a guard in front of me and one in back, I entered an upper chamber and was amazed at how intricately artisans had painted the walls with obelisks, winged griffins, lotus leaves, flowers, and aquatic plants.

Augustus had his back to us. When he turned around, his piercing blue-gray eyes fixed on me as he seated himself behind a large wooden table with neatly stacked scrolls. He motioned for me to continue standing.

Stealing a glance around the room, I found it odd that my mother was not there, but instead, two guards stood on each side of the closed door. Augustus's eyes probed me for a moment before he began.

"Do you know why I summoned you here?" he asked.

I could not boldly tell him that I anticipated his support for my position as praetor, so I prudently responded as my mother had always advised when speaking with a powerful ruler.

"Perhaps you can enlighten me," I answered but immediately questioned myself on whether I should have been more direct, as my father often instructed.

Augustus picked up a scroll from the table-top and smoothed out the parchment. "This is a request for me to support your position as a praetor in the justice system."

I exhaled the breath that I had been nervously holding. At that moment, I felt more relieved that Janus was, indeed, opening a new opportunity for me.

Augustus tapped the parchment on the table. "Give me a good reason why I should support your lofty ambition for such a position. You are not yet eighteen."

"Your eminence, my tutors will attest that I am a skilled orator and a most loyal Roman citizen. Therefore, I am most willing to be mentored by whomever you choose so that I may serve you," I declared boldly.

Augustus set the scroll down and clasped his hands on the table. "I've been slow to respond to your request because I have had to deal with treasonous acts in my inner circle." His stern expression prodded me for a response.

Baffled, I fumbled for words. "Um, I'm so sorry, but…but I am unaware."

"The grandson of Marcus Antonius doesn't know, does he?"

I jerked my head back. Augustus had never before mentioned my grandfather's name in my presence.

Augustus took in a deep breath and exhaled slowly. "Well, how do I say this so you understand what loyalty entails?"

His comment sounded like a threat to me. As he continued, I searched my mind for what I might have said or done to offend the elderly statesman.

"Let me start at the beginning of my tale when I showed mercy. There was never a more traitorous Roman than your grandfather. I could have had his children who were not of my bloodline executed," Augustus emphasized with a slam of his hand on the tabletop. "But I did not."

Anxious about the direction the conversation was heading, I suddenly felt lightheaded and could feel the pulse pounding in my neck. I wavered on my feet, trying to maintain balance.

"You look pale," Augustus commented, feigning concern. "Do you want me to continue?"

What else could I do but agree? My voice cracked. "Please do."

Augustus leaned back in his chair; his eyes fixated on me. "Of course, I had to consider that Marcus had been married to my sister, Octavia. May she rest in peace. But Marcus betrayed her and his commitment to Rome when he divorced her and married the Egyptian sorceress. Does your blood boil with his betrayal?"

Dumbfounded, I could not answer. My mind continued to wrestle with what I might have done to incite the ruler's ire. I wiped away the hot sweat dripping down my face.

"Oh, sweet Octavia," Augustus moaned. "There was not a more faithful and dutiful wife than her. She begged me to spare all of Antonius's children. I spared your father, Iullus, yet I could not spare his brother, Antyllus. He sealed his fate when he chose to fight alongside his father."

Augustus lowered his eyes and rubbed his forehead as if trying to calm himself. "Your mother is so like Octavia…a devoted wife and mother, do you not agree?"

I could barely swallow before replying. "Indeed."

"Surely you have sensed the tension between your parents," Augustus said, his stare staked on me again.

I only nodded because of the lump forming in my throat.

His eyebrow raised. "Did you not wonder why your father has not returned home?"

A sick feeling churned in my stomach. With my mind focused on obtaining Augustus's patronage to support my position as a praetor, I had not considered that my father had done something to draw the ruler's attention. But I could not fathom what it was.

I stumbled for words. "Yes. But...but all married couples have issues at one time or another. Do they not?"

Augustus's expression softened. "You do not know, do you?"

A sob clutched my throat. I looked away, misty-eyed, so I would not risk humiliating myself by showing weakness. I took a deep breath to compose myself before turning back to Augustus. "Forgive me, sire. Would you enlighten me as to what has happened to my father?"

"Before I do so, you must first answer a question," he demanded.

"Of course," I replied, sensing the heat from the ruler's blazing eyes.

"Do you swear your fealty to me?"

I had enough wits about me to quickly answer him in a stronger voice. "Yes. I swear my utmost loyalty and allegiance to you as my sovereign and patron."

Augustus gave a slight nod of what appeared to be his approval of my answer. "As a praetor, will you prosecute all traitors and enemies of Rome with utmost vim and vigor?"

"Yes, of course," I declared. "I swear to serve you honorably. I will prosecute your enemies as if they were my own."

"I will hold you to that oath, Lucius Antonius," Augustus replied. "Guards!" he shouted, abruptly rising from his seat.

Panic set in as the two guards rushed toward me, drawing their swords.

"I do not understand. Am I under arrest?" I asked, horrified.

Augustus leaned across the table. "A secret court has condemned your father to death as a traitor. Do you still vow to serve me without hesitation and prosecute my enemies like they were your own?"

I stared in disbelief, not comprehending why my father would betray such an influential figure who had elevated him like a son. We were part of the imperial family. My father was married to the eldest daughter of Octavia, Augustus's sister. My father had held influential political positions—he'd been a praetor, a consul, and an Asia proconsul. He had lauded Augustus as the preeminent political figure that had made Rome the wonder of the world.

Augustus's brusque voice drew me out of my desperation to grasp what treasonous act my father could have committed to deserve death.

"Were you so blind that you didn't see what your father was doing behind your mother's back?" he asked, a biting edge to his voice.

I felt like a helpless slave rebuked by his master. My voice quivered. "I swear on Jupiter's stone that I do not know what my father has done."

Augustus grimaced and clutched his chest. "Your father broke both your mother's heart and mine when he openly committed adultery with my daughter, Julia. Only the gods above know how many men Julia has bedded. I am banishing her for disregarding my moral laws. I am also banishing the men who copulated with her. But not Iullus," Augustus growled through clenched teeth. "Not a son of Marcus Antonius, whose name I have forbidden to be spoken in public. No descendant of the most treacherous man in the history of Rome will lie with my daughter and live!"

I felt as if someone had ripped my guts out—as Augustus might do to my family's legacy, my future. And I had not yet proved my worth as a young man. The image of Brigata's expressionless face etched into my mind, and the sound of her voice saying, *"A slave has no rights,"* made my anger bubble to the surface.

I am not a slave. I am a noble with the right to a trial with a judge.

I brashly defended myself as if I were in court. "How can you condemn me for my father's actions? I am also of your blood. Remember. My mother is your most beloved niece."

Augustus's brow creased. "All that, I know too well. Did I say the court condemned you?"

I stepped toward the table. "No. But you insinuate that I will be held accountable for my father's wrongdoing."

Each of the guards gripped an arm to restrain me as the white-haired princeps stepped closer to me. His eyes blazed as he brusquely admonished me. "I warn you but once. Do not jeopardize your standing and go down the same pathway as Iullus. The reason I summoned you and your mother, who is waiting downstairs, is to tell you that your father has agreed to commit suicide instead of being publicly executed. In turn, I have agreed that your family will not be forced to forfeit his property to the imperial coffers but will be allowed to keep it. But only under certain conditions."

I bit my lip at the stipulation of "certain conditions." Augustus had undoubtedly given my father the option to take his life honorably in order to spare my mother the anguish and humiliation of her husband being executed like a common thief. Yet, deep down inside, I recognized that my mother was the sole reason Augustus had spared me from my father's fate.

"What are these conditions?" I asked.

Augustus cocked an eyebrow. "You will soon learn. Your mother awaits us in the Room of the Masks. An apt place for me to say my final lines in this family tragedy."

3

Room of the Masks

MY LEGS FELT LIKE A lead weight as I descended the staircase to the main floor. Although the two guards escorting me were dressed as citizens, I knew beneath their togas were hidden the fangs of their weapons, ready to strike me down if I tried to escape. Brigata's image and her words about not having a choice about my destiny continued to plague my mind. As I marched down the colonnaded corridor past closed doors to other rooms, I kept my eyes focused on the foreboding entry to the Room of the Masks.

A stern-faced guard clicked the door open, allowing me to enter the chamber where artisans had painted the walls with vivid red and yellow colors to give the illusion of entering a wooden theatre structure. Ghostly tragic and comic masks gawked at me from their box seats on either side of the stage. Above the painted room was a coffered ceiling that appeared to be an integral part of the theatrical illusion. My mother stood in front of the stage, dressed in a black tunica and stola, back turned with her hair loose. She slowly turned and looked vacantly into the distance.

I felt like a spectator gazing at a tragic figure, my mother standing center stage. Her face was pale as white marble, her eyes red-rimmed from weeping. A sob rose in my throat, but as a Roman man, I could not display a woman's weakness. I hardened myself and fought off tears. I had to stay strong as the tragedy played out.

My mother's eyes reached out to me, but she stayed frozen like a statue as Quintus and his armored guards escorted Augustus into the chamber. It was clear from the presence of guards in military uniform that Augustus did not trust how I would react when he announced the conditions for our family to retain our personal property. His pack of armed wolves was ready to pounce on me if I made any untoward move.

Augustus exchanged glances with Quintus. I stepped to the painted stage and lightly kissed my mother on her cheek.

"I am so sorry," I whispered.

Her fear-struck eyes widened, warning me to be cautious.

A slave entered with two chairs and set them down before the stage. Augustus offered my mother a seat next to him. The praetorian prefect gestured for me to stand beside my mother.

Augustus leaned over and patted her hand. "As you can see, Marcella, no harm has come to your son."

"Thank you. You have been most gracious to me," came my mother's meek reply.

I could feel my jaw clench, knowing my mother had consented to her uncle's demands, whatever they were.

A young male slave entering a side door drew everyone's attention as he set a jar of wine on a travertine table near the back wall. He poured wine into two goblets, diluted it with water, then stepped over to Augustus and my mother, handing each a filled vessel.

The slave offered me none.

When I glared my displeasure at Augustus, Quintus, sensing my anger, gripped my arm and pulled me back between the two guards who were fiddling with the hilts of their swords. Seeing the praetorian prefect's scowl, I lowered my eyes to avoid any conflict.

Augustus finished his wine, then stood in front of the theatre stage and adjusted his toga. His eyes were fixed on me as he spoke.

"Marcella, no one is dearer to me than you. Though you have begged me to spare Iullus, I cannot. His betrayal strikes at my heart. Though he denies he ever plotted to overthrow me, both my daughter's and his actions indicate otherwise. When Julia asked to divorce Tiberius to marry Iullus, I told her that I could never agree to such an arrangement. Iullus is already married to a dutiful, chaste, and honorable wife. I believe your husband tricked Julia into believing he loved her so he could fulfill his ambition to rule Rome."

When I saw my mother lower her head, I knew she struggled to contain her tears before responding. Her voice was weak. "I accept that my husband is a traitor and deserves to die for what he has done. But I beg mercy on my son, Lucius."

Augustus's glare pierced through me. "Sons avenge murdered fathers, do they not?"

My mother stole a glance at me. Though I could not hear her thoughts, her eyes pleaded that I beg for Augustus's mercy even though I had done nothing wrong. Had I not been brought into the theatre room to enact my part in the family tragedy?

Every word said by the man I considered a tyrant was like a slow-acting poison robbing me of my dignity. I swallowed my pride. "No, my gracious eminence. I will never avenge my father. On the contrary, it is my duty as a Roman citizen to defend you against all enemies that have betrayed you."

"How can I be sure you will keep that promise?" Augustus's eyes probed me like a scalpel.

"I will do whatever you ask of me," I replied, immediately regretting the words once I finally heard Augustus's conditions.

"To demonstrate your loyalty, you must witness your father's suicide."

It felt like a brick had punched me in the stomach. All the air sucked out of my lungs. Every muscle in my body went numb. I could not grasp the reality that I would have to watch my father die in disgrace. Though he'd never paid me the attention I sometimes craved, I was nonetheless from his loins. I was his flesh and blood.

"I will do what you ask," I said with a quavering voice.

"You played your part splendidly and must continue to do so. Now for the final act. Guards are escorting Iullus from the dungeon to his home as we speak. There, Quintus and four of his guards will serve as witnesses to his death, as will you. No slave will do the deed for him. Only you can assist him," he said, a thin smile on his lips.

Every muscle in my body wanted to charge and strangle the life out of the cruel monster standing before me, but my mother's widened eyes warned me not to act out. I could feel my jaw tighten as I said the words that tore at my heart. "If that is what you command, I will do it."

Enraged, I wanted to gouge his bloodshot eyes that kept probing me, but I refrained and put on a mask of stone. At that moment, I was but a common slave forbidden to make choices. There was nothing I could do to save my father. I had to abandon my conscience and do what the stage director demanded. If not for myself, for my mother. She had suffered the humiliation and anguish that my father would soon die.

Augustus gave his final orders. "Take Lucius home to fulfill his role in the last act. Marcella will stay with me to plan for the private funeral rites."

Augustus offered his hand to assist my mother up, but she stiffened. I wanted to reassure her that everything would be fine and that I would remain strong for her. Yet, I recognized Augustus had staged the events to test my loyalty to him. I could not imagine the conflicting emotions of anger, shame, and disappointment tearing at my mother's heart. Finally, the praetorian prefect and his guards forced me to leave the illusionary theatre and march down Palatine Hill to witness the final tragedy.

4

Forced Suicide

THE GUARDS LED THE DEATH march with burning torches in their hands. I fought with my inner soul about the abhorrent choice that I was about to face. Augustus Caesar was the imperial paterfamilias with godlike powers of life or death over me. *If I do my moral duty as a son to defend my father, I lose my life. If I remain silent and yield to the cruel emperor, I lose my soul, my reason for living.*

I had never seen Augustus so unhinged. He had always been manipulative and controlling while wearing a mask of propriety and sound reasoning in public. But he had overreacted to my father's improper conduct with Julia. My father did nothing more than what other men in the ruling class secretly did. They pursued passions outside of marriage, following the advice of Ovid in his poem *Ars Amatoria* ("The Art of Love"). Ovid did not believe in paying for sex but rather enjoyed hunting down married women for his pleasure as he proclaims in his poem:

> *All we need is your consent to some*
> *quiet love-making—*
>
> *It is hard to imagine a more harm-*
> *less request.*

"A harmless act that will cost my father his life," I mumbled to myself.

I contemplated why Augustus had chosen to reveal my father's treason to me as a dramatic tragedy. He must have lashed out for reasons other than Julia's defiance of his expectations of what constitutes the epitome of a chaste wife. The princeps had exceeded the penalties for adultery specified by his legislation. How could misconduct between the sexes be construed as treason?

I recalled seeing Julia in the forum when I celebrated the Bacchanalia festival with Gaius Caesar one night. We hid behind a column and watched her place a wreath on the head of the statue of Marsyas—a satyr and companion of Bacchus whom the Greeks referred to as Dionysus. In the Greek myth, Marsyas challenges Apollo to a musical contest with the lyre. Apollo loses and punishes Marsyas by skinning him alive.

Gaius and I shrugged off what Julia had done, though she did not have permission to do it. My father had told me that the Greeks regarded Marcus Antonius as a reborn Dionysus. The statue of Marsyas wore a Phrygian cap, a conical headdress characterized by a pointed crown that curls forward. Freed slaves wear these caps on their heads to symbolize their independence. Was Julia's act of placing a wreath on the satyr's head a protest against the repressive demands of Augustus, who was, in essence, a tyrannical emperor?

The clap of the lion-headed knocker brought me back to the reality that my home, where I had transformed from a boy to a man, would be the site of my father's forced suicide.

Panic suddenly gripped me. I rammed my shoulder into one of the guards in a foolhardy attempt to escape the upcoming horror of watching my father slice his abdomen open.

A second guard shoved me so hard that I fell and slammed my face into the cobblestone, making my ears buzz. A knee dug into my back, robbing me of breath, and someone yanked my wrists up to tie them together, then pulled my head back by the hair and pressed a razor-sharp blade against my throat.

"Decide now. Life or death?" the praetorian prefect's voice growled.

The instinct to survive kicked in as the blade pressed harder on the lump forming in my throat. Finally, I no longer resisted and went limp.

Strong hands rolled me over onto my back like a slaughtered pig. Quintus's face lowered next to mine, his lips touching my ear.

"Do it again, and I will cut out your intestines and burn them in front of you," he whispered threateningly.

The pulse in my throat beat so rapidly, I feared I would pass out. Quintus yanked me to my feet and pushed me through the open doorway.

Inside, household slaves were corralled at the front of the atrium. From within their midst, Brigata's fear-struck eyes reached out to me. The guards gripped my arms and dragged me through the atrium to the torchlit peristyle garden, where the fragrance of crimson roses overwhelmed my senses.

I was thrown face-down on the gravel pathway in the garden. Dazed, I spit out grimy dirt and sharp-edged pebbles. The bridge of my nose pounded as I lifted my head and gasped for breath.

There before me, my father was on his knees. "Do not resist," he cautioned.

Struggling to keep my head up, I could see that the guards had battered my father. His left eye was swollen almost shut; black and blue bruises discolored most of his face. Clots of blood clung to the thick, dark hair that he had taken such pride in grooming. This tragic figure looked nothing like my father, Iullus Antonius. A handsome man even in his forties, he had been the epitome of a masculine noble with smooth, olive skin, a strong chin, and thick lips. His hazel eyes had a hint of a green glow under bright light, and his boyish smile lit up the room whenever he greeted his guests.

My father's voice was firm as he spoke to the praetorian prefect. "Please untie my son. He needs to hold the sword steady as I fall on it."

I wanted to cry out, *"Don't make me do this. I refuse to help you die,"* but I ultimately had no choice in my father's fate. He was a condemned man. He would either die by his sword honorably or face the disgrace of public execution. I fought back the tears as I laid my head back on the rough surface while they untied me. My arms jerked as the rope holding my wrists was sliced with a dagger. Finally freed from my restraints, I pushed myself to a crouching position and looked up at the praetorian prefect. "May I stand?"

Quintus nodded, but his guards were in a ready position with their short swords in hand. Staggering to my feet, I took a deep whiff of the lavender scattered throughout the garden and coughed from its irritating smell. It felt as though my body had disconnected from my mind, and I had entered a dream state. Everything seemed to occur in slow motion as the next moments unfolded.

"Say your final words, Iullus," Quintus demanded.

"Tell the gracious princeps," my father began, "that I willingly atone for my treason against him with my death. I am guilty of disregarding his moral laws and not pursuing politics with due gravitas. Even so, I never conspired to do bodily harm to him or rebelled against his authority. My only intent was to assure the smooth transition of power from Augustus to

Julia's sons, Gaius and Lucius, whenever the gods took him."

My father turned to me. "Help me, son, to die with dignity. Tell your mother that I am sorry for the shame I brought upon her and our family. Serve Augustus Caesar with utmost loyalty. Do not follow my path. I serve as Augustus's avenger for my crime and am ready to die."

The praetorian prefect handed me a gladius with a ridged wooden handle that allowed a firm grip. Under the watchful eye of Quintus, I placed one knee on the ground to stabilize myself. I held the handle of the gladius steady on the pebbled pathway with the tip of the blade pointed toward the moonlit sky. As I gazed at my father's watery eyes, I knew that I could never live with myself if I helped him to die.

I dropped the sword and rose to my feet. "I refuse to be part of my father's execution!"

Two guards immediately gripped my arms to restrain me as Quintus stepped next to my father and glowered.

My father clasped the hilt of the gladius and studied it for a moment. "Promise me that no harm will come to my son for his refusal to assist me," he demanded.

Quintus's lips pressed in a firm line. "I promise as long as you open your stomach and spill out your guts."

My father's eyes shifted to me. "Augustus has sealed my fate, but not yours. You must survive and rise out of the ashes of our family's scandal."

I slightly nodded to acknowledge my father's charge. The only way I could avenge his death was to live and regain our family's legacy.

My father knelt on one knee, took a deep breath, and pushed on the handle of his gladius. I could sense his pain as he forced the blade into his abdomen and sliced it upward. When his intestines began slithering out of the wound and his blood spurted on the gravel pathway, he keeled over on his side, still gripping the hilt of his weapon. In obvious pain, he moaned and squeezed his eyelids shut as if willing himself to get past the agony. He inhaled deeply and prayed in a faltering voice.

"Remember me," he muttered.

Clasping the hilt of the gladius, my father drove the blade up to his chest. His eyes widened in the throes of death.

A brisk breeze reminded me to breathe when my father took his last breath. Both rage and grief consumed me. In my heart, I inwardly swore that I would never forget that my father, Iullus Antonius, had risen to the pinnacle of political power only to fall because of slanderous lies. With the reality hitting me that he had taken his own life, I wanted to curse Janus for looking the other way, for closing the door on my father, my family, and me. Yet, to strike vengeance now would doom both my family and me. I could only avenge my father's death by staying alive and restoring my family's name.

Quintus placed two fingers on my father's neck and closed his eyelids. I knew then, my father had joined Marcus Antonius and his elder brother, Antyllus, in the tranquil fields of Elysium. The stars and moon whirled around me like glittering dust. Shadows lurked behind columns in the peristyle.

My mind shut down. I felt numb. My teeth clattered from the chills.

Quintus spoke, "I've sent a messenger to tell Augustus that Iullus is dead. You will stay here for the night and clean off the remnants of death. But, of course, we'll need to keep the guards here. The slaves will prepare his body for funerary rites. I will send for your mother and sister tomorrow after the priests have purified the grounds of evil spirits."

Loud bangs of a hammer chiseling stone made me wince as I walked under the roofed peristyle to return to the main household. Under a torchlight, one of the household slaves was chipping away at the stone face of my father's statue—an act of *damnatio memoriae*. The image of my father as an astute statesman reciting poetry in a purple-striped toga leaped into my mind.

Father, I will never forget you.

5

Aftermath

THE MOON WAS AT ITS zenith when the guards escorted me to the private bath. I was rattled. My hands shook as I stepped into a candlelit room with a marble bath. I gaped in horror at the sight of bright red bloodstains on my hands and clothes.

Brigata was there, waiting for me. She washed the blood away from my face and hands with a wet cloth, then unwrapped my bloodstained toga and disposed of it in a woven basket. After helping me pull the sticky tunic over my head, she undressed herself and clasped my hand. We both stepped into the bath's tepid water topped with rose petals. As a nearby guard leered at her, she sponged off the crimson evidence of my father's death. Sensing her discomfort, I glared at the young guard, who then shifted his eyes away from Brigata as she finished washing me.

Brigata wrapped a new cloak around me and put on a gray tunica. Then, like a mother, she held my hand as we passed the guard, whose stare followed us to my bedchamber where another armed man stood guard.

I removed my cloak and dropped it on the floor. Brigata blew out the candles as I lay naked on the bed, watching her until darkness enveloped the room. She snuggled against my back, and I turned to nestle my head next to her soft breasts, seeking warmth and comfort.

"I'm so sorry," she said, caressing the top of my head. Her lips found mine in a deep kiss, my pent-up grief releasing like floodwaters as I began to weep, leaving traces of my tears on her face and neck. It was not a moment of passion but one of vulnerability, something a master and a slave seldom share. Was I not like Brigata?

A slave at the mercy of a Roman tyrant with the power to crush my destiny?

"I'll stay with you tonight," she said softly, holding me tightly in her arms until fatigue conquered me, and I fell into a deep sleep.

⁓

The next day, the praetorian guards outside my bedchamber did not allow me to leave. Only Brigata was permitted to bring me food and assist me with my black toga for the funeral. It unsettled me that I did not know what funeral rites Augustus would allow for a disgraced noble.

Quintus informed me at noon that my mother was still making funeral arrangements from Livia's villa, where she and my sister, Iulla, had stayed overnight. Therefore, no visitors would be allowed into our home until my mother arrived later.

In midafternoon, a guard announced that my mother had arrived. Quintus and one of his guards escorted me past my father's shrouded body that lay in state on an ornate, raised bed set in the middle of the atrium. His feet pointed toward the door. Linen covered his head except for his face.

I was surprised to see my father's half-sister, Matron Antonia, accompanying my mother and Iulla into the atrium. Matron Antonia, the daughter of Marcus Antonius and Octavia, was another highly regarded niece of Augustus. Since her husband, Nero Claudius Drusus, had died while battling in Germania years ago, she had displayed undying loyalty to her uncle. And although Augustus had pressured her to remarry, she never did.

Due to my father's disgrace, I assumed that nobody from the imperial family would be allowed to view his body except for the immediate family. Perhaps the princeps had taken pity on my mother and allowed Antonia to comfort her. I doubted Augustus extended the courtesy to other males from the imperial family. I wondered how my friend, Gaius Caesar, had reacted to his mother's banishment. Would he be forced to discontinue his friendship with me?

I greeted each woman with a kiss on the cheek, and we silently walked to my father's body. A sob caught in my throat when I observed that the thick lead makeup did not mask the bruising on my father's swollen face. My mother appeared dazed as she gazed upon the corpse before her.

Matron Antonia placed a hand on my father's pale forehead. "Go in peace," she whispered

My mother's voice, filled with emotion, cracked. "Oh, Juno, sweet goddess above. What have they done to his face?"

Antonia embraced my mother. "I am so sorry. He was such a striking man," she said soothingly.

Iulla joined the two women in an embrace as they openly cried. During the awkward moment, I did not know what to say or how to comfort them. Women were free to shed tears, but I was not. Weeping was a sign of weakness for a Roman man. Furthermore, Quintus would construe my grief for my father as disloyalty to Augustus. I was delicately dancing on shards of glass.

After the women released each other, my mother looked at Quintus with pleading eyes. "Would you please remove your guards so we can mourn in private?"

Quintus's stare hardened. "Augustus ordered that all guards are to stay here until the funerary priests remove his body tonight."

"You can keep your guards outside the entrance or in the garden until the undertakers take my husband's body," my mother suggested. "If you do this favor, I will speak highly to Augustus about how you treated me graciously during this difficult time."

The prefect's expression softened. "We'll keep the guards outside until his body is moved this evening."

It surprised me that Quintus conceded to my mother's request. Perhaps it was because she was still in good favor with Augustus, despite my father's disgrace. The princeps may have empathized with my mother because my father also betrayed her.

After the guards left, my mother clasped my hand and pulled me into her arms. "I am so sorry," I whispered in her ear for the second time that day.

Misty-eyed, my mother patted me on the chest. "Let us talk privately in the small meeting room at the back."

Excusing ourselves, we left Matron Antonia to console Iulla while we went into a small room sparsely furnished with a table and two chairs. There, my mother finally disclosed her true feelings.

"I feel so torn. I must grieve for Iullus but also accept that he committed adultery. Everyone else in the family circle is too scared to pay their respects to your father. I have never seen Augustus so unbalanced. He has isolated himself and refuses to speak with me. I do not know what he plans to do with you," she said sorrowfully.

I did not know how to respond to my mother. As the eldest son, I was now the pater-familias, but I felt powerless.

"Let us see what the next few days bring," I finally said.

"Do not do anything that will turn Augustus against you. Hide your anger and yield to his commands," my mother warned.

"I will never forget Iullus Antonius was my father. I will never—"

"Do not speak his name again," my mother demanded. "Not if you wish to flourish."

I turned away to hide my anger. *I refuse to erase my father's memory and destroy our legacy!*

My mother gripped my hand. "Did you hear me?"

I glared at her. "I heard you, Mother. I have no choice but to wait for Janus to open another door, do I?"

We returned to the atrium. Iulla, weeping uncontrollably, turned to me, seeking my comfort. "I will always be here for you," I assured her.

We silently viewed my father's body, now an empty shell of the charismatic poet and statesman I remembered. There would be no public ceremony to recognize his accomplishments. No one from the family would be present when his body burned on a pyre. I assumed a herald would announce my father's suicide and treasonous act to the public. After that, Augustus would damn his name and erase it from the public records. The descending sun's red glow was as brilliant as the sunrise when I anticipated Augustus's patronage to elevate my political standing in Rome.

In the early evening, the undertaker and funerary assistants carried my father's body to a hand-drawn cart to be moved outside the city gates for cremation. I gazed at the crimson-tinged clouds of the sunset as the rhythmic clacking sound of the cart's wheels faded into the distance.

After Quintus and his guards finally left at twilight, the women went into my mother's bedchamber, leaving me alone in the atrium. When I asked the porter where Brigata was, he told me she was in the kitchen. I thought it best not to summon her, as it would upset my mother to see me with her.

Wearily, I sat on a stone bench and gazed at the pool. Beneath the surface of the water, I could see the mosaic of a chariot race, reminding me of the bet I had won and the promise that Janus would open the door to my political future. Unfortunately, that dream was now beyond my grasp. I would need to pay the price for my father's indiscretion.

Startled by a sudden tap on my shoulder, I turned to find a man with a white toga pulled over his head that hid half his face. Recognizing that the toga was typical of a Praetorian Guard member, I jumped to my feet, ready to defend myself against an assassination attempt.

"Calm yourself," the man said, uncovering his head. Then, to my shock, I recognized my lifelong friend Gaius Caesar. He gave me a hug that took away my breath.

"I cannot stay long," he said, urgency in his voice. "I had to conceal my identity so nobody would see me come here."

Taken aback, I stared at him. "I am glad you came. But are you not risking your grandfather's ire?"

"Of course, I am," Gaius said. "My grandfather is so angry that he has lost all emotional control. He has isolated himself and refuses to speak with family members or me. On behalf of Augustus, a quaestor read a letter today to the Senate that highlighted charges of treason brought against my mother and her so-called lovers for violating the *Lex Julia* moral laws. My mother will be banished. A judge condemned your father to death as one of her lovers. Later, my grandmother told me that your father had already taken his life. Is it true?"

Overwhelmed with emotion, I could barely speak the word. "Yes."

Gaius's eyes widened. "How could Grandfather do something so heinous? Yet, if I protest, he could do the same to me. He has put pressure on me as his heir. I must do everything he commands."

"What does this mean for me?" I asked, suddenly apprehensive that the princeps could execute me for my father's indiscretions.

"Get out of Rome if given the option," Gaius urged. "Start a new life elsewhere. Stay out of politics. As for me, the old man chains me to his dreams and legacy."

"Will I see you again, friend?" I asked sadly.

"It is best that we're not seen together for now. Let us see what pathways Janus opens for us," Gaius said, pulling his toga back over his head, a signal that he had to leave.

We embraced each other for what might be the last time.

6

Sunrise

As Brigata and I held hands and strolled along the shoreline of Massalia, I remarked about how the water sparkled like turquoise diamonds under the rising sun. In the distance were three islands, landmarks of the bustling coastal city in southern Gaul. Though my grief and anger had somewhat abated, I remained bitter about what Augustus had done to my father.

Shortly after the funeral, my mother showed me a will that Marcus Antonius had secretly delivered to my father before committing suicide in Egypt. Marcus Antonius had vowed to build and dedicate a temple to Mars after his glorious victory at the Battle of Philippi to avenge Julius Caesar's assassination. Thus, as the heir of Marcus Antonius, my father was obligated to build the temple of Mars Ultor, which was finished after my father's suicide. However, Gaius Caesar and his brother Lucius had the honor of managing the games to celebrate the dedication of the Temple of Mars Ultor instead of my father.

I suspect my father's implication in Julia's adultery was political, not a sexual issue. Might Augustus have considered my father a threat if he were to dedicate the temple in the name of Marcus Antonius and redirect the glory from the princeps to his hated rival? Like that of Marcus Antonius, my father's true motivation for his liaison with Julia will remain a mystery.

Mother stayed silent about how she felt about my father's death. Everyone in the family had to mask their true feelings. Sometimes I feared my repressed emotions might erupt into vengeance.

I kept reminding myself that Augustus could cut me down like a stalk of grain and harvest me with the other traitors. He gave me the choice of exiling voluntarily to Massalia as an alternative capital punishment to death. If he had banished me, I would have forfeited my citizenship and property.

Brigata's laughter drew me out of my contemplation. Running back and forth with the waves on the beach, she did not seem to have a care in the world. As a Roman noble, I had never thought I could love a slave. Brigata comforted me while my noble friends abandoned me like the plague. I was more a slave to my political ambitions than she was a slave to me.

I had wrestled with the prospect of whether she could truly love me if she remained my slave. The only power I had left was to set her free.

And today would be that day.

I excitedly pulled the document from a belted pouch and handed it to her. "Open it."

"What does it say?" she asked, unrolling the scroll.

I smiled. "It says you are a free woman."

Brigata clutched the parchment to her chest. "Does it mean that I can leave at any time if I so choose?"

"You can choose whatever door Janus opens for you," I replied.

As for me, I must grudgingly accept my fate that Janus closed the door for my ascension in the Imperial Court, forcing me to exile as a pariah to Gaul for my father's crimes. Yet, the god of beginnings opened another portal for me to study law in Massalia under the mentorship of a renowned judge.

Janus had not yet sealed my future. I vowed to keep the promise to my father that I would survive and open another door to restore my family's legacy out of the ashes of Rome's maligned heroes.

Please leave a review for
TWO FACE OF JANUS
Keep up-to-date with the latest
news from Linnea Tanner
at https://www.linneatanner.com

Author's Note

The family dynasty of the first Roman Emperor, Augustus Caesar (often referred to as the princeps), reached a crisis point in 2 BC as various factions in the family maneuvered to shape the politics after he died. Augustus had only one biological child, Julia, with his second wife, Scribonia. He divorced her to marry Livia, who brought two stepsons (Claudian dynasty) into their marriage but never bore a child with him. Augustus used Julia as a political game piece to assure the Julian dynasty through strategic marriages. The Antonius dynasty was added to the mix through Marcus Antonius's marriage with Augustus's sister, Octavia. The inner turmoil finally culminated in repercussions that assured that Livia's son, Tiberius, would become the ultimate heir to Augustus.

One of the mysteries in Roman history is why Augustus Caesar overreacted when he learned Julia had adulterous affairs with influential politicians. The penalties he carried out on his beloved daughter and her supposed lovers far exceeded the severity of those in his moral legislation established in 17 BC. Julia's primary lover was Iullus Antonius, the son of Marcus Antonius (Mark Antony). Augustus forced Iullus to commit suicide for treason while he banished the other lovers of Julia for their indiscretions. Forced suicide was considered a more honorable option for an aristocrat because public execution resulted in the family's forfeiture of property to the imperial government. In addition, there was likely a political element of infighting between two factions—one centered on Julia and her sons (Gaius and Lucius) and the other on Livia and her son, Tiberius.

One of the accusations leveled against Julia is that she put a wreath on the statue of Marsyas—a satyr and companion of Dionysus. She prostituted herself during her late-night adventures. Her actions may have been an anti-government demonstration calling for the return to Rome's lost freedoms under Augustus's rule. Marsyas's association with Dionysus evoked the memory of her lover's father, Mark Antony. Julia might have headed a political faction dedicated to promoting her sons' interests as successors to Augustus instead of Livia's son, Tiberius.

History is silent on how Iullus's wife, Marcella Major, and their eighteen-year-old son, Lucius, reacted to his suicide and disgrace. Marcella Major, the oldest daughter of Octavia, was first married to Marcus Vipsanius Agrippa—Augustus's close friend, general, and statesman responsible for constructing some of the most notable buildings in the history of Rome and for critical military victories. After Augustus almost died in 23 BC, he forced Agrippa to divorce Marcella Major to marry Julia. The political marriage between Agrippa and Julia strengthened the constitutional stability by providing for a political heir or replacement if Augustus succumbed to his chronic ill health. Marcella Major was then obligated to marry Iullus Antonius, and together they had one son, Lucius, and a daughter.

Historical accounts say little about Lucius Antonius except that he went to Massalia (present-day Marseilles) on the pretext of studying law after his father's disgrace. Likely, Augustus unofficially demanded that Lucius voluntarily exile for his father's crime. There are no accounts of how Julia's sons with Agrippa (Gaius and Lucius Caesar) reacted to their mother's banishment. Both of them died tragically in their twenties, resulting in Augustus designating his stepson, Tiberius, as his heir.

Two Faces of Janus is based on actual historical events. Still, the details are fictionized to dramatize the family tragedy that ensued due to Augustus's cruel actions, prioritizing his political power over his love for the family.

Acknowledgements

I am grateful to those who have supported me on my continuing journey as an author. In addition, I'd like to acknowledge my long-time critique partners who provided feedback on the plot and characterization in this short story—Kate Anderson, Thomas Goodfellow, Ryanne Buck, and my husband, Thomas Tanner. One of the challenges I faced is whether Lucius Antonius would assist in his father's suicide. I finally decided against it based on their feedback.

A special thanks are extended to my editors, Marilyn Burkley and Nonnie Jules, for providing me valuable feedback from their thorough line editing. Also, I would like to acknowledge Kathy Meis and Shilah LaCoe from Bublish, Inc. for their invaluable advice and assistance in print cover formatting, internal formatting, and distribution. And finally, I appreciate the contribution of 4WillsPublishing Author Services for their cover design.

About The Author

Award-winning author, Linnea Tanner, weaves Celtic tales of love, magical adventure, and political intrigue in Ancient Rome and Britannia. Since childhood, she has passionately read about ancient civilizations and mythology, which held women in higher esteem. Of particular interest to her are the enigmatic Celts, who were reputed as fierce warriors and mystical druids.

Depending on the time of day and season of the year, you will find her exploring and researching ancient and medieval history, mythology, and archaeology to support her writing. In addition, she has traveled to sites described in her books. Books released in her historical fantasy series, ***The Curse of Clansmen and Kings***, include the following: ***Apollo's Raven*** (Book 1), ***Dagger's Destiny*** (Book 2), and ***Amulet's Rapture*** (Book 3). ***Skull's Vengeance*** (Book 4) is anticipated to be released in late 2021 or early 2022.

A Colorado native, Linnea attended the University of Colorado and earned both her bachelor's and master's degrees in chemistry. She lives in Windsor with her husband and has two children and six grandchildren.

To keep up-to-date with the latest
news on her upcoming books,
please visit and sign up for
her FREE newsletter:
https://www.linneatanner.com/